# SIX GOOD ENDINGS

## A Short Story Novelette
## by
# Joe Roubicek

*Six Good Endings*
*Copyright 2025*
*Joe Roubicek*

GILBERT
STREET
PRESS

Illustrations,
Book & CoverDesign
PDKingDesign.com

# TABLE OF CONTENTS

# WHY I WRITE

My family has inspired me to write since childhood, although my mother and big sister could sometimes be discouraging. They constantly corrected my grammar and punctuation, but as English teachers, they couldn't help themselves.

I have forgiven them.

Uncle Bill was a different story, however. He would fire up my imagination with animated stories like the Vegetable Man, a strange creature with a carrot nose and broccoli tail that lurked in the woods by my home. Aunt Dorothy inspired me through her accomplishments as an editor for DC Comics.

This was my inspiration then, but what keeps me writing now?

When I put memoir on paper, it becomes a kindly reminder of where I came from. Events become endearing reflections of childhood experiences despite the challenges.

Fiction is my avenue to create stories in settings where anything is possible. But it has to be palatable enough for the reader to buy it (As I did the Vegetable Man, staying clear of the woods by my home.)

My stories are seafaring by nature because I grew up on the waters of Long Island. The Great South Bay, the Long Island Sound, and the Atlantic were all playgrounds that created good memories and fiction.

After college, I moved to Florida for a stint in the Navy, then a career with the Fort Lauderdale Police Department and State Attorney's Office. My downtime was often spent diving along small coral reefs on the east coast, where I would be joined by sea turtles, manatees, and, on one occasion, a very persistent bull shark.

All these events made for good fiction. The following stories are some of my favorites. I hope you enjoy them.

# THE HOUSE (MEMOIR}

*I was* born and raised in a convent until the Sisters of Seton Hall sold it to my family. It was located in the Village of Patchogue on the south shore of Long Island. Like Quogue, Setauket, Montauk, and Shinnecock, Patchogue is a Native American name, not easy to spell; it means "a turning place," and for our family it was.

Our family was poor, as were many others during the 1950s, and my parents had their hands full with seven children. I would be the eighth, the "surprise baby" who would come along another five years down the road, and my father would move out shortly after that. Not a rosy picture, but life doesn't have to be easy to be wonderful.

The old, three-story Victorian was located just two blocks north of the Great South Bay where I spent much of my childhood days treading clams, feeling for them with my feet in the sandy shallows, or fishing off what we called the "L Dock" for its shape. There were six bedrooms in the house, each with a sink in the corner, so I believed that bedrooms normally had sinks. I never used them because the water was clouded and rusty; but as a child, I could picture the nuns dressed in black washing up at those sinks, all quiet, mysterious, and a bit spooky, to be honest.

Just before the Sisters of Seton Hall sold the house to my family, they moved a grave off the property, that of Sister Clotilda, a former Mother Superior of the convent. She was re-interred from our backyard to a location elsewhere, and my mother spoke about this as if her spirit was still present, making our house and its grounds uniquely spiritual. This didn't help my childhood view that the dead once lay where I played. The yard was my playground, after all, and I couldn't picture Sister Clotilda playing war games with me and my little green army men playset.

All this talk of spirits and graves had me thinking our house was alive. I don't mean that it would come alive like in horror movies or Looney Tunes, but that the house was alive as in a being, a living thing—it just acted up sometimes.

On calm summer days, I could feel the house relax and imagined it quietly taking in the bay breeze. When winter storms lashed out and pipes burst or the cellar flooded, I saw my house as being injured and distressed until repairs were made.

On windy nights, I would hear things that I could usually understand. These sounds had rational explanations, like creaking wood, doors closing by the breeze, the furnace firing up, or a hot water pipe rattling. But sometimes I would hear things that just didn't make sense, especially on those quiet nights when everyone should have been asleep. My bedroom was on the second floor, and at times I could hear the distinct sounds of wooden chair legs sliding coarsely along the old linoleum floor in the kitchen downstairs. I assumed it was my siblings. Most of them were much older and had the freedom to come and go as they pleased, as long as they were quiet at night for our working mom. When I questioned them, though, they denied being up then and blamed it all on my imagination. But I knew this was not the case. "I'm young but not stupid," I thought. So I just listened to the house's normal chatter.

One night, when the sounds of the sliding chairs woke me, I slipped out of my bed to the head of the stairway and looked down to see a dim glow coming from the kitchen. I sat down on the top step and waited. The chairs stopped moving, but I heard faint whispering from the kitchen, then silence, and more whispering until I was sure that my siblings were up. Tiptoeing slowly down the dark stairway, I reached the bottom only to see that I had been mistaken. The kitchen was empty. Four chairs sat around the kitchen table as the streetlight's reflection shone in through the window. If it had been my imagination at work, then things were exactly as they should have been, but this troubled me. I was sure of what I had heard, and the only possible explanation was ghosts.

The next day, I spoke to my mom about this. I needed clarification of what was real and what was not—fact or fiction. The kitchen was Mom's favorite room. When she wasn't at work, Mom would sit at the table reading paperbacks while snacking on crackers and Muenster cheese peppered with . . . well, lots of pepper. On weekends, she'd have pigs' knuckles and sauerkraut slow cooking on the stove, and she'd purr to her noisy parakeet in its cage on top of the refrigerator. I could tell this was her happy place.

When I told her about what I'd heard the night before, Mom didn't tell me that I was imagining things as I thought she would. She peered over her reading glasses and said, "We live in a hallowed place, and there are only good spirits here." Then she went back to her book.

She said it so matter-of-factly, as if I should have known this, and that was completely unexpected. How could I argue with someone who agreed with me? I accepted what she said, and her words seemed to validate my belief that our house was alive as well.

I believed that spirits are real, and this must be spirituality. One that seems to have no boundaries.

That was six decades ago. To this day I don't have a rational explanation for the moving chairs on the tiled kitchen floor, and I like it that way. It's a reminder that sometimes spirituality can conflate fact and fiction just enough to keep my life interesting.

I have so much to learn.

# SWAN RIVER  (Memoir)

*I was* thirteen when we sat on milk crates under the twilight. A glow rose behind dark clouds in the eastern sky. Aside from the sounds of whispering snowfall, chattering teeth, and a distant whistling of duck wings, it was a quiet dawn. I could smell the bay, the marsh, and although my hands and feet were numb, that didn't matter. I was happy to be by the river's mouth—it did that.

"Joey, stop chattering," Phil whispered.

"I c–c–can't," I replied, "too c–c–cold."

I was beside my three brothers behind a thin wall of cattails and felt like a real man with a hunting permit on my back. We had to be very quiet because mallards were skittish that time of year.

"Duck season," John whispered.

"Wabbit season," Ralphy replied.

"Shut up!" Phil scolded.

Hunting was different back then. When you're poor, game is food, and I didn't feel so bad with this in mind. Duck, rabbit, pheasant, or fish caught on a line or in a net was food for the table. We had no boat, so our decoys sat just offshore. We tossed them from land, and a connected clothesline kept them from floating away.

As daylight set in, the whistling wings became more prominent. We could see flocks flying over the bay in the distance until a band of six mallards finally swung in low to join our decoys. Just as they were landing, we filled the air with gunshot blasts, and only one didn't fly away. I knew it wasn't mine because I hadn't fired the instant it fell, and Phil quickly claimed it. Neither Ralph nor John challenged him, so it was Phil's to fetch.

"Better him than me," I thought. "That water's cold."

I followed my brothers from behind the blind to the shoreline, where we watched the catch slowly drift away from the decoys with the outgoing tide.

"Joey, go get the duck."

I looked at Phil incredulously. "What? No! That

water's freezing."

He laughed. "C'mon, don't be a baby. Get out there before it drifts away."

"No! C'monnnn," I whined.

"Joey, be a man. Get out there now. Go!"

In that moment, I knew Phil wouldn't make me go if I continued to refuse. He was a protector, and without a dad around, that's what big brothers do. When John and Ralph joined him, cajoling me to "be a man," I knew I had three protectors, but still, I was cold and the bay was much colder.

I couldn't bear the thought of being "a baby," so I set my gun down and walked through my comfort zone into the water. As the bay entered my boots and crawled up my legs, I could hear my brothers cheering me on. When the water rose above my waist, I wondered if my penis could freeze off. When it reached my chest, I became breathless and realized that my entire body was numb. I felt no pain, and it really wasn't that bad because numbness can be better than pain. Looking back, I wonder if this is when I considered feeling numb as a good protection. If so, I wish I could go back to correct that.

I grabbed the duck and quickly turned back toward shore, where my brothers were still cheering me on. If I were Jewish, this would have been my Bar Mitzvah, a rite of passage. It was a transition not unique to the mouth of Swan River, where the river's current joins the bay's tide.

During summertime, the bay brought snapper, weakfish, and blue crabs into the river for good fishing, and we all treaded for clams just outside the inlet. My sister Emily was twice my age, and she brought her children along with a dragnet to pull by hand just offshore. They kept everything too. Even the shiners tasted good when fried in butter on a skillet.

Being a bit older, I could spend more time by the river with friends rather than family, and naturally, this is where my first kiss happened. I forget the girl's name but remember one thing: you can smell a girl when you kiss her. It's like when you smell a puppy, but she didn't smell like a puppy. And although we never passed first base, I felt like I had hit a home run. The kiss did come back to haunt me though.

\*\*\*

I don't know why, but I never attended kindergarten. So I struggled from day one of first grade through the fifth, when I was finally held back, and this was a blessing in disguise. I was finally able to get my bearings academically, no longer drawing the ire and wrath of the sisters of Saint Francis de Sales Elementary.

It was a tough school. The nuns slapped my face for looking at them the wrong way, and I could only imagine what they would have done in response to an eye roll or smirk. I had two uniforms per year, and my pants had iron-on patches over the knees because I rarely changed after school. Mom was always at work, so I did things my way.

Passing at Saint Francis required a grade of at least seventy-five, so when I found out that the public junior high school just across the street had a passing grade of sixty-five, I was jealous. The junior high only ran from sixth to ninth grade, yet it was four times the size of our school. I heard that rebellion was tolerated over there, and they didn't have to wear uniforms. All the more reason for me to want public school, but Mom made it clear that wasn't happening.

Normally I stayed away from the junior high, with one important exception—what I called the Fight Club. Even the name was cool. One kid would call out another, word spread, and an after-school match would be planned in the open field behind their building. After school each day, I would walk to the deli across the street for candy, and if a crowd gathered behind the junior high, I joined them. I was shy and didn't know many of the public–school kids, but the fights were more like sporting events, and it felt good to be part of the crowd. In those days, everyone was poor, some poorer than others, and I felt more comfortable with the latter.

The Fight Club became a popular regular event. Dozens of kids would show up to root for the opponents, while a few of the older kids—the "alpha males" among us—kept things organized. They would dictate when the fight began, though sometimes when it ended, the winner was still pounding away on the loser coiled up on the ground.

Fighting was different back then, more about honor than revenge. Fights involved only fists and wrestling until a winner was on top and loser on the bottom. A bloody nose was cool, and when both had bloody noses, even better.

One ominous day, I bought my candy at the deli and followed the public–school boys to the field, but as I drew closer to the crowd already gathered, I realized they were looking back at me—all of them. It felt awkward in my Catholic school uniform with those patches on my knees until I heard a familiar voice yell, "Hey, Joe!"

A girl ran from the crowd, and it was that girl— the first one I had kissed by Swan River. I still can't remember her name.

"You're going to fight today!" She grabbed my arm and gave me a big smile as if I had just won something.

She explained that another boy had been picking on her, so she told him that her boyfriend from the Catholic school would kick his ass.

"But I'm not your boyfriend," I said.

"Just for now, pleeease?" She leaned against me.

Panic set in as one of the alpha leaders called out for my opponent.

"He's not here," someone said. "Took the bus home, but said he'll fight tomorrow."

"Same time, same place tomorrow, folks," the alpha leader said as the crowd whined and dispersed.

The girl leaned on me. "Don't worry, Joey. You can beat him. He's not that big." She kissed me on the cheek and walked away.

My fear grew without mercy as I walked home. I had been in fights before, and when I'd lost, it hadn't been so bad. I'd felt sorry for myself and moved on, but this was different. It was the crowd I feared, the possibility of total humiliation that could last forever. Home was a mile away, giving me plenty of time to consider ways out of my predicament, but to no avail. Not showing up would make me a coward and surely disappoint my brothers.

That evening, my imagination ran wild until bedtime. I pictured myself bloodied, pinned down to the ground by my opponent's knees. He would be laughing as the crowd cheered, and that girl would be gazing down on me sadly. I would never kiss her again or show my face without shame at the Fight Club.

So I did something I had never done before. My brothers weren't around, so I went to my mom, who had gone to bed early because she had to be up before dawn for work.

Standing in the hallway, just outside her open bedroom door, I couldn't see her face because she liked to place a towel around her head to keep warm. I told her everything and asked her what I should do.

She was quiet for a while beneath all that cover, and then she told me to say my Hail Mary prayers so things would work out. This was not the answer I sought. My life was surrounded by religious dogma, and my mother's first name was Mary, with her maiden name Grace. I knew that all the "Hail Mary, full of grace" in the world would not lessen the blows of my opponent.

Retreating to my bedroom, I felt angry with Mom at

first, but even at that young age, I realized how tough her life really was—keeping a roof over our heads and food in the fridge. It became my predicament again, not hers, and I resolved to deal with it myself.

After school the next day, I walked straight past the deli and continued behind the junior high into the field where the crowd was waiting. I was still afraid but determined. Thoughts of humiliation gave way to facing the music and doing my best. The girl greeted me with more words of encouragement, which helped a little. As she walked me into the middle of the crowd, I realized she was the only girl around. That's one of the things I liked about her: she was like one of the guys, except very pretty.

Time passed, and after fifteen minutes without my opponent appearing, someone walked up and shouted that he wasn't coming. He had been seen taking the bus home. Relief washed over me as an alpha–male leader patted me on the back, saying, "Looks like you win, Joe."

"That's it?" I asked.

"That's it," he said.

It was over that fast, too fast for all my worry.

The girl walked me home, leaning against my side from time to time, talking endlessly about what a jerk the other kid was. It occurred to me she was very manipulative, and I began to think she probably scared the hell out of my opponent. As for me, I'd just kissed her by the river and look what happened.

That evening, when my mom got home from work, she didn't ask me how things had gone. Perhaps I didn't look any worse for the wear. Instead, she ate dinner at the kitchen table while reading a paperback and then watched television for an hour and went to bed.

My mom was all about survival—that's what life was for her. Not the best message for a young person, but there was truth in it at the time.

As for the Hail Mary prayers, who knows? Maybe they worked. The alpha leader just said, "You win," and I became a member of the Fight Club without swinging a fist.

A life lesson formed that day: sometimes you win, sometimes you lose, and sometimes what you fear never happens—and all that worry was for nothing.

# THE HIDDEN

*The* boy sat awkwardly on his pew, feet dangling above the floor as he tried to sit back, so he leaned forward and held on to the seat. His father used to call him "runt," and each time his mother had countered that he was gifted. "You don't need this," she'd say, patting the muscle on her arm, "just this," pointing to her head, "and of course this" patting her heart.

The boy missed them both very much.

A priest stood behind the altar dressed in green and gold reading aloud: "Revelationes, Ego sum Alpha et Omega, primus et novissimus, principium et finis…"

The boy did not speak Latin but recognized the words from bible study: "I am the Alpha and the Omega, the

First and the Last, the Beginning and the End."

How can God be everywhere all the time and all at once? the boy wondered. God is elsewhere, not here.

It was a chilly April Sunday morning in the Northeast when blooming chestnut trees adorned the sidewalks of Eatons Neck, Long Island, where winding two-lane roads, summer cottages, and potato farms lined the east end.

But inside that church, the boy scanned the rows of pews with pathways for entry and escape. He thought of his father, a carpenter, who said the small knots scattered here and there on the wooden surfaces were once branches. The tinges of red and pink lines along the lacquered wood were once rings. "Count the rings," his father used to say, "and you can tell the tree's time."

The boy spotted an unusual knot. It was light-colored, surrounded by halos of disk-shaped, white-banded rings, like a tiny elongated, milky white smudge.

***

Elsewhere and many years later, April mornings were bright and warm with calm trade winds as two men with salt-and-pepper hair and Hawaiian shirts loaded two sets of scuba gear and three full coolers onto a fiberglass skiff. In the port of Isla Mujeres, a small island eight miles east of the Cancun coast, the two friends were beginning a tropical vacation they'd talked about for years, a well-deserved break from their ongoing research. Sunshine, palm trees, mojitos, reef dives, adventure. Five miles further east, a reef known as "Caves of The Sleeping Sharks" awaited them, where carnivorous creatures rested motionless in its caverns.

Their boat, a rented twenty-five-foot Boston Whaler powered by a 250-horsepower Evinrude, was more than enough to venture safely into the Caribbean.

Thomas stepped behind the boat's console while admiring the Whaler's design with sleek curves from stern to a broadened, rising bow. Scanning the harbor, jade fading into bright blue, Thomas could hear the ocean just beyond like a conch shell to the ear. He hadn't been on a dive in years and he felt a rush of gratitude that John had pushed it to the top of the bucket list.

Thomas turned the key. A ping followed a high-pitched whizz; then the engine kicked in with a low, powerful hum.

"Everything okay?" John asked.

Thomas turned the engine off, waited, and turned the key again. This time it kicked in instantly with a smooth, steady rumble as if wanting to be cut loose.

"Yep, everything's fine," he said. "Untie us, mate."

Thomas revved up the Evinrude, and the boat pulled away from its mooring. As they idled the inlet, Thomas entered the reef's coordinates into the console display screen, a broad, multi-function display with GPS, depth finder, and radar for weather.

Sophisticated, he thought, then smiled, recalling childhood fishing trips with his father in a tiny wooden skiff on a bay. His mother would scold them when they came home late to a cold dinner. His parents were a complementary pair: Dad a source of fun, Mom the protector. He missed them. They weren't really gone, but he missed them just the same.

***

It took thirty minutes, though it felt like only three when they arrived at the beacon buoy that marked the reef's edge.

The anchor sat on top of a neatly coiled pile of rope. John tied its end to the cleat, then tossed it into what appeared shallow water until the line continued to zip down into the sea.

"How deep?" he asked.

"About forty feet." Thomas said, "You look nervous. You sure about this?"

"I'm sure," John said, "and I'm excited, not nervous. You look nervous."

"I am, dammit."

Methodically, they put their gear on while neither spoke. Buoyancy compensator vests with weight pockets went on first, followed by tanks and fins. Sitting in the ready with backs to the water, they gave each other nods, a "thumbs up," and plopped back into the sea.

John led the way down, and Thomas followed. The clarity of the deep took him, his sounds of inhales, exhales, and the freedom of weightlessness made him feel as if he had entered into another dimension.

The curtain of blue haze opened to a reef where coral castles sat high on colorful ridges. They swam by colonies of small fish: red-lipped blennies, crimson damselfish, blue angels, and bar jacks that flashed silver. Below the castles were cliffs of older grey coral, mostly dead. Within these were the caverns.

Reluctantly, Thomas followed John into the first opening, a short tunnel that led to a dark chamber with a single beam of light stretching down from the top. They carefully made their way through the room to discover other tunnels leading to more caverns, some well-lit, others dark and foreboding. As they explored the maze Thomas felt relieved that there were no sharks to be seen. There were few fish for that matter, and soon Thomas felt comfortable enough to wander off on his own.

He spotted a nurse shark about five feet long, tucked inside a dark crevasse. He knew them to be passive and drew closer. The creature appeared to be sleeping with its eyes open. It's only movement, small whiskered jaws that slowly opened and closed.

Reaching out, he touched its sleek, flanked torso. He noticed that it had smooth skin, not sandpaper-like, and gently he began to pet it. Almost instantly, the fish bolted from its crevasse and darted for an exit. As it flanked Thomas, its tail slapped his head just enough to set his mask ajar and fill with water. His eyes stung, and he impulsively swam upward, then banged his head against the coral ceiling. He struggled to stay calm, knowing what panic would mean. Then he breathed evenly through the regulator, readjusted then cleared the mask. Quickly at first, he swam for the nearest tunnel. The sting on his head reminded him to slow down and, as he paddled into the next chamber, he was relieved to find John waiting.

John gave him two thumbs up and Thomas responded in kind. Then John pointed to the top of his head. A translucent red swirl dropped into Thomas's view.

Thomas pointed upward, and together they swam for an

exit to return to the boat. The cavern had several, but John grabbed his arm when Thomas tried to exit the closest. A grey torpedo-shaped torso with a white belly and blunted nose swayed just outside. Thomas recognized it instantly, an aggressive bull shark with a stout body that gleamed in the sunlight, both beautiful and terrifying, as it passed by disappearing into the blue haze.

John pointed to a ledge on the opposite side of the cavern, and they crossed together, but Thomas paused at the opening as tiny trails of blood continued to pass by his view. He looked at John, who understood, took the lead, and exited into the light. Thomas followed.

Emerging from the reef, Thomas looked upward to see the sun's reflection on the ocean's surface just thirty feet above. Now he panicked, knowing both safety and danger were seconds away as he rushed upward past John.

It didn't take long before a small, juvenile reef shark the size of a barracuda darted out front and bolted for Thomas's head. He extended his arm instinctively and pushed its head to the side, but the juvenile was fast and persistent. It spun, snapped, twisted and finally latched onto Thomas's leg. Dozens of tiny daggers crushed down in a burning microsecond. He pushed the shark and punched helplessly as the sea turned red. The pain abated as he drifted into shock.

He saw John swim back down through the clouded water, then behind him the silhouette of a bull shark. The bull was slow at first like a battleship, then it knocked John aside and sprang in quickly. While it may have wanted Thomas, the bull chomped down on the reef shark, and Thomas watched helplessly as its chainsaw teeth slashed down, then side to side, as its eyes rolled white. The shark's five-hundred-pound torso then knocked Thomas aside as it swam away.

\*\*\*

Thomas opened his eyes as John shook his shoulder and he looked down at his right thigh, half wrapped in a red-stained white towel. The pain was sharp and relentless as if his thigh was still clamped in the shark's jaws.

"How bad is it?" he asked.

"It was shaking your leg pretty good," John said. "I expected far worse."

After the blood-soaked towel was removed, Thomas was surprised by the ferocity of his pain from small, eight-inch semicircles of narrow puncture wounds. Blood oozed slowly from each puncture.

While John poured tequila over the area, Thomas bellowed obscenities he hadn't used in years, but after his leg was wrapped and the job was done, the compression and remaining tequila eased his pain. As his head cleared, he remembered the sharks, John pulling him to the surface, flopping over the boat's stern, then nothing.

"Are we back in port?" Thomas tried to stand up and collapsed.

"No, stay down. The engine won't start."

Thomas's heart raced. Shark bites have bacteria.

"C'mon, help me up," Thomas said. "Let me try it."

"No."

"John, let's go!" He held up his arm, and John reluctantly placed it over his shoulder then helped him to the console. Thomas turned the key, and a loud, rapid click sounded, then faded to a slow tapping until there was just the sound of waves lapping the bow of the boat.

***

Hours later, they sat quietly side-by-side, watching the sunset spread beams of gold light onto the Caribbean until John finally broke the awkward silence.

"Where the hell were the sleeping sharks, anyway?"

"I saw one," Thomas said. "Nurse shark sleeping in

one of the crevasses."

"Really ... big?"

"Pretty big. Slapped me in the head with its tail. After I petted it."

"You petted it?" John laughed.

Thomas smiled. "I guess that wasn't the best option."

It seemed to John that Thomas was looking better.

They sat quietly until the sun faded to the west beyond Mexico. The breeze cooled, and Thomas shivered. John helped him back to his bed of towels with backpack pillows, where he fell into a deep sleep.

During the night, John opened his eyes to a star-filled, half-mooned sky. Something was off. He heard the breeze, felt the boat sway, but something was different. Then he realized the boat was rocking, and a dreadful thought came to him. The anchor rope that he tied, not Thomas, was gone. He scanned the area for land or a ship. Thoughts raced through his head, and he dropped to his knees.

"What's going on, John?" Thomas's eyes were open now, gazing at the stars.

John looked down. "We're adrift."

Thomas sighed and said nothing.

"I'm sorry I pushed you into this, Thomas. Sorry about

the sharks, the attacks, the anchor, everything."

Thomas got on his elbows next to an empty tequila bottle. "Help me to the side; I need to sit up a bit."

Once there, he looked at John. "I'm a big boy, John. You didn't talk me into anything, and honestly, this whole thing has been pretty exciting." Thomas raised his finger, "It's not death a man should fear, but never beginning to live."

"Shakespeare?" John asked.

"Marcus Aurelius."

Thomas turned away and heaved. It was a dry heave, and when he turned back his pallid face dripped sweat and his lips quivered.

John reached out, "C'mon, lie down, too much tequila, my friend."

Thomas pulled away. "It's not the tequila."

John carried him back to the makeshift bed and Thomas lay back watching the stars.

"You want to know what I fear most?" Thomas asked. "Being alone. Not adrift in the Caribbean, but alone, and right now, I'm under God's stars with my best friend, Besso."

"Too much tequila, Einstein."

John watched him as he shut his eyes, then closed his own just for a moment.

***

In the early light of dawn, John spotted a distant boat beyond the gentle morning waves. His heart pounded as it drew closer and he made out a rickety, wooden skiff pushed along by a tiny outboard engine sputtering silty clouds of smoke. His shoulders dropped.

Sitting in the stern were an old man with sunbaked white hair and a little girl, maybe fourteen or so. Her long black hair matted against her head as she leaned against his shoulder.

"Saludos Señor," the old man shouted as they motored up. "Es Bueno verte."

John could see their boat was taking on water through its planked bottom. A supply of food, water, and a folded canvas tarp sat by the bow.

"Buenos dias," John greeted them. "Do you speak English?"

"Yes," said the girl standing up now, hands on her thin hips. "We speak well. Can you take us to land?"

John leaned over, grabbed their bow, and took the rope from its cleat.

"Sorry, we're stranded. Looks like we're in better shape than you, though. You from Cancun?"

"No," said the old man as he began handing supplies up to John. "Honduras."

"Honduras! We're in the Gulf of Honduras?"

The man laughed. "No, we traveled north through Mexico, bought this boat to cross over to Cuba, and maybe America." He spread his arms. "But the boat has different plans. We're maybe fifty miles east of Cancun. I am Pablo, and this is Lucy."

"Welcome, Señorita." John helped her aboard the Whaler.

Pablo looked at Thomas. "You do not look well."

"I don't feel well. A shark nipped me in the leg."

Pablo knelt by him and opened the dressing. The gashes on Thomas's thigh had swelled into deep red and puffy white ridges, with pink veins extending downward.

Pablo spoke to Lucy in Spanish and pointed to a small green duffel bag. She brought it to him, and he pulled out a sealed plastic baggie holding dark green, blade-like leaves with pointed ends. Breaking open the leaves, he squeezed a clear gel-like liquid into Thomas's hand.

Thomas winced as he lightly tapped the liquid along his wound.

"So, how are you stuck?" Pablo asked. 'We have petrol."

"We have plenty of gas," John said. "Battery's dead. It worked fine when we left Isla Mujeres."

Pablo leaned over the big Evinrude, released a latch under the lower side, and swung the top half of the engine's cover outward. The massive engine head, its large, flat steel flywheel two and a half feet in diameter, was surrounded by electronic components and covered by long, black rubber strands.

"Alternator belt broken," Pablo said. "Probably when you left Isla Mujeras." He pointed to a round metal object on the engine's side with a smaller flywheel. "This charges your battery. No belt, no battery. Is this your boat?

"No, we rented it," John said.

"Good," said Pablo. "Then there is a search party. Now we wait." He looked at Thomas. "They'll find us. Do you have a flare gun on the boat?"

John and Pablo went to the front of the boat and opened a latch door to the bow compartment while Lucy sat down beside Thomas. She studied his wound while tilting her head.

"Does it hurt bad, Señor?"

"It doesn't feel good, but it looks worse."

"Mi padre was a doctor," she said. "I will be doctor one day."

Thomas was about to ask the obvious, but Lucy's expression stopped him. She was small again, distant.

"I'll bet he was a wonderful doctor."

"Si." Her eyes swelled with tears as she looked out on the Caribbean, quietly mouthing words he could not understand. He could feel her detachment, a silence louder than the waves or the commotion at the bow. Then with a sad smile, he recognized himself in her. Orphans are special, he thought.

"We have a medical kit, a flare gun, and three life preservers," John said from the bow.

"Only three?" Thomas said. "How fortuitous, John."

"Don't worry, pal. We won't need 'em."

***

By late afternoon they sat side-by-side beneath the tarp splitting the last sandwich and Pablo's dried fish, and plantains. Thomas ate little but drank water as the Tylenol from the medical kit relieved his fever and pain.

"So, Lucy, is Pablo your grandfather?"

Her smile faded as she looked at Pablo, "We are two amigos, like you and John."

"Sorry, I didn't mean to …."

"That's okay, Señor," Pablo said. "Ask anything. We are tired of running now."

"So, you're not just migrating?"

"No, refugees. We flee." Pablo's tone lowered, and Lucy placed her head against his shoulder.

"Soy agricultor de cafe," he said. "I farm coffee for Antonio, Lucy's father, for many years. He was a very good man, a doctor. He helped everyone in the village, including me. But farm is gone now, everything gone, muerto. Criminales come, banditos, drug dealers. They want to share Antonio's farm for poppy, but he say no. They threaten him, and he tell la policia. Then banditos come at night and burn casa, but they not see me. I stop their capitano with machete."

He looked down. "I could not save Antonio." Lucy leaned into him, and he put his arm around her. "We run. They follow. We get to Mexico. Still, they follow. Then I buy the boat."

They sat quietly, then Pablo asked, "How about you two amigos?"

"We're a couple of physics professors on vacation from New York," John answered. "And our dream vacation turned into a nightmare at a reef called Caves of the Sleeping Sharks." He looked at Thomas. "They weren't sleeping."

"Physics?" Lucy asked.

"Yes. We study the universe," Thomas told her.

"Everything from subatomic particles to the stars, like the sun up there."

Lucy pointed to the sun, "The closest star."

"That's right. "Ninety-three million miles, or just eight light-minutes away."

"Light-minutes," she said. "Space-time."

John gawked at her, and Pablo laughed. "Lucy and her father would look at the stars with a telescope. She knows the stars. Ask her anything."

She smiled. "Galileo saw the stars with his telescope."

"That's right," Thomas said, "and he discovered the Milky Way was made of individual stars."

"Sí, Milky Way, Via Lactea."

"Well, it looks like we have a child prodigy on board, John."

Thomas shivered. His leg was swelling, the Tylenol was wearing off, and he welcomed her distraction.

"Lucy, did you know that time is the fourth dimension?"

"Sí," she stood up and waved her hands, "There is left and right, up and down, forward, backward, then time, the fourth dimension." She pointed at the sun, "Eight light-minutes away, Thomas."

"Then you know of Albert Einstein?"

"Si, he was an immigrant like us." She sat proudly, and he studied her.

"I think we have a lot in common, señorita," Thomas said. "I lost my parents in a car accident when I was younger than you. I miss them very much. But I think that my thoughts of them are not just memories, but connections, thanks to Einstein and the stars."

Lucy scowled a little. "I don't understand."

"Einstein believed that we live in a universe where everything is connected. Time is a dimension—linear like a straight line. The distinction we see of the past, present, and future is just an illusion, although as he said, a very convincing one. So, the past still exists on that linear, straight line, and so do they."

She took it in. "I still don't understand."

"In his universe where everything is connected, the existing past grows with the present as time moves into the future."

"Nonsense, the past is gone," Pablo interjected.

Thomas ignored him. "Lucy, picture yourself standing on the road in front of your farmhouse. Then you walk down the road until you can't see the farmhouse anymore.

Does that mean it is no longer there?"

"No," she said.

"Like your house, the road behind you is still there even though you can't see it. That's the illusion of time."

"So," Pablo said, "could Lucy walk back to the farmhouse?"

"No," Thomas admitted.

"It would take an act of God, right señor?"

Thomas shivered. "Probably."

"Then farmhouse gone. Past gone. Good to leave it alone."

"Past not gone, Pablo. It's just … elsewhere. Best word I've got for the moment."

Thomas looked to the west where the sun was setting on the horizon.

Lucy laid down using a towel as a pillow. "You believe your parents are down the road?" she asked.

"Yes."

"Señor," Pablo whispered. "You mean well, but tragedy is in the past. Look to future, have faith. Better than science."

"Theories take faith, Pablo, and what if God is the universe?"

"Then maybe God is time." Pablo stretched out, resting his head on a backpack.

***

It was still dark. Thomas watched the moon pass, then Aries and the North Star. He made out the others sleeping along the deck and felt grateful for their company.

His chest was heavy, but the wheezing had stopped. He remembered a sickly childhood after his parents left—having bronchitis, then pneumonia, with fever dreams of spinning away from a cluster of stars into space.

But now the stars know of me, and I of them. I can handle anything, he thought.

He looked at John, his lifelong friend lying by the console, then little Lucy, the prodigy child, and Pablo, the protector by her side, who was right; after all, if God is the universe, then God is time.

His body was shutting down but he found peace knowing friends surrounded him beneath the cosmos. He spoke to the stars. "Let that child know she is not alone. You took so long for me," and closed his eyes.

In time, a spray of seawater crossed the deck. It awakened everyone.

Pablo sat up first then slowly made his way across the

boat. He and the others gathered around Thomas. "How are you, amigo?" He placed his hand against the nape of Thomas's neck.

Thomas smiled. "No problemo, Pablo."

Pablo sighed. "Still a sense of humor."

Lucy squeezed gently past the men and sat down next to Thomas. She took his hand into hers. He looked upward, and she followed his gaze to a faint, milky band of glowing light just above the horizon.

"Oh, Via Lactea, señor!"

"There it is," he said, "where everything is connected."

"And the past is not gone," she said. Then she looked into his eyes. "You said it would take an act of God to go back. You know what God would say?" She squeezed his hand, "I love you, Thomas."

He choked with emotion. "And there it is."

Then he saw it—a ship's beacon on the horizon. Closing his eyes, he heard the waves lapping and felt the boat's rhythmic motion. *God cradles me with the sea.* Thomas inhaled the salty air and felt the lulling breeze and, still the scientist, observed how his brain selectively chose what to allow and deny. His final thought was of his childhood — a church pew.

In his universe where time is an illusion, where one can feel loved and live forever, where Galileo discovered the Milky Way, as Einstein formed his theory of relativity, as a little boy sat elsewhere in a church on Long Island where the chestnut trees were taken by blight fungus, and potato farms were replaced by vineyards while the roads stayed, there the little boy heard Latin chants echo off hallowed walls: "I am the Alpha and the Omega, the First and the Last, the Beginning and the End." He smiled, lonely no more, and pointed to a milky streak on the back of a church pew whispering, "Via Lactea!"

# THE GOOD PROSECUTOR

*"All* rise," said the bailiff. "Existential Court is in session. Judge Maggie Temple presiding."

John O'Malley watched the judge enter briskly from the chamber door and take her seat behind the bench. She looked familiar, attractive too, he thought.

John sat, stunned to find he was at the defendant's table. Who was he defending? There was no one beside him. On the other side of the courtroom, the prosecutor took a sheaf of papers out of his briefcase.

John scanned the empty gallery. The room reminded him of church, with wooden pews and a judge who sat on an elevated platform that looked a little like an altar. He eyed the prosecutor shuffling papers on his table and thought he was not a bad-looking fellow. Then he remembered that prosecutors could become persecutors, depending on their intent.

A good prosecutor pursues a just outcome, while a persecutor only pursues a win.

John refocused his wandering thoughts on the matter at hand. How had he gotten here? And what had the bailiff said—Existential Court?

Judge Temple glanced his way and, as if reading his mind, explained the court's proceedings briefly. "This court handles only personal matters, and especially matters of the mind. We're a timeless place where past, present, and future coexist as needed," she said.

John swallowed hard but nodded his understanding. He'd been in countless courtrooms in his life, but this was a new one. "Your honor," he began. "If I may, who is the defendant?"

The judge's gaze softened. "Why, you are, Mr. O'Malley."

Drawing in a deep breath, John looked around the courtroom again, searching for any face that might be familiar. The prosecutor caught his eye, expressionless. John looked away first, then noticed the tall windows behind the empty jury box. Through the glass he saw snow falling in huge feathery flakes, drifting earthward in a soothing pattern.

John pressed his hands against the tabletop in front of him, feeling the solidness of it. He didn't know how he had gotten there, what the charges were against him, or why he had to defend himself. Making me a fool for a client, he thought.

\*\*\*

"So, counselor, what's the charge today?" the judge asked. "Authenticity? Despair? The meaning of life?"

"Not good enough," the prosecutor said as he stepped before the bench.

John sat back in his chair. Oh, you've got to be kidding me! He'd beat this handily.

The prosecutor continued. "John O'Malley is forty-three years old with a wife, Mary, and a young boy named Thomas."

That's when it registered in John's mind—the judge looked like Mary.

"They've been married for fifteen years, churchgoers living under honest and modest means. He's a career man who works long hours with dedication to his job while serving the community."

The judge looked at John and smiled. "Oh, one of them." Then she pointed to the witness stand. "Have a seat, Mr. O'Malley, and raise your right hand."

After John was sworn in, the prosecutor wasted no time. "So, John . . . may I call you John?"

"No," he said. "I think we should stay professional here."

"That's fine, John," the prosecutor said. "Now for starters, tell me about your son, Thomas."

"What does my son have to do with this?"

"It's a simple question. You're his father."

"That's right—and he's the most important thing in my life, everything any dad could want. He's bright, innocent, curious." John smiled, "When I look at him, I see myself, in a way. I'm proud of him."

His eyes drifted back to the courtroom windows just for a moment. One overly large snowflake caught the breeze and made a loop in the air. John's smile widened as he recalled a snowball fight with his son years ago.

"You're a lucky man," the prosecutor said. "He just turned eleven, right?"

John snapped his attention back to the prosecutor. "Yes, a month ago."

"And when he asked you to volunteer to coach his soccer

team last spring, did you?"

"No," John said. "Would have loved to, but work made that impossible."

"And when he asked you to take him to a ballgame? Chaperone his school trip just before Thanksgiving?"

He knew where this was going. "My career requires my complete dedication and commitment for the sake of the community. My son understands that and so does my wife." His eyes darted to the judge, who had the same habit of pursing her lips as she listened—just like Mary. "And, if I may be so bold, I'd think that, as a prosecutor, you would understand this as well."

The prosecutor narrowed his eyes a fraction. "But I'm not the one facing this charge—you are."

Then, turning to the judge, the prosecutor announced he was ready for his next witness.

Judge Temple instructed him to take his seat, and John stepped down from the witness box.

"Your Honor," the prosecutor said. "I would like to call Johnny O'Malley to the stand."

Sighing, John started to get up. What kind of games were they playing here?

"Not you, Mr. O'Malley," the judge said. "Sit down."

"Your Honor, this is absurd," John protested. "And 'not good enough' is not a crime."

"May I remind you that this isn't criminal court," the judge replied. "Existential Court handles different matters. Now, please sit down."

The bailiff opened the courtroom door and a little boy with blond matted hair, wearing a soiled Yankee jersey, walked down the aisle. He smiled at the defendant as he passed.

John half-rose out of his chair to watch himself as a child approach the witness stand. His mind filled with memories and his eyes with tears as he recalled being that child. He fought the urge to hug that boy and tell him that he was safe, that everything would be okay.

"Have a seat, young man," the judge said in a softer tone.

"Good morning, Johnny," the prosecutor said, smiling kindly. His demeanor changed as well with the boy, and John appreciated that.

"Good morning," the boy said.

"And how old are you?" the prosecutor asked.

"Eleven."

"Same as Thomas." The prosecutor shot a look at John. "You're a young man already. I'd like to hear all about your family. Let's start with Dad—his name is Bill O'Malley, right?"

The boy nodded.

"And what does Mr. Bill O'Malley do?"

"He lives in a camper in the outdoors, the woods and all."

"But what does he actually do for a living?"

The boy hesitated. "I don't know that much about him. I just see him sometimes on the weekends."

"How about your mom—Sharon? What does she do?"

The boy smiled. "She's a teacher at a high school in another village."

"Really. Teaching is an important job."

"Yep. She has to drive a long way and gets home after supper sometimes, when she has meetings and stuff."

"So, who's there when you get home from school?"

The boy paused. "No one."

"How do you feel about that?"

"Mom says she keeps a roof over our heads and food in our stomachs," Johnny replied.

"Yes, yes, but she does other things as well, right?"

The boy thought for a moment. "She was in a bowling league for a while. She's the president of a church club—and she's helping my friends get first communion because their moms have to work too. She's pretty busy."

"She sure is," the prosecutor said. "But what about you? I mean, why isn't she spending more time with you?"

The boy hesitated. "It's just the way it is. My mom's not a bad person."

"Not at all. Like you said, she's very busy, and mom is always right."

"Yes."

"But if she doesn't have time for you, what does that say about you?"

John O'Malley stood. "Objection! Your Honor, he's leading the witness, putting words in the mouth of a child."

"What clichés would you like me to use, then, Mr. O'Malley?" the prosecutor shot back, his voice rising. "She did the best she could? Her intentions were good?"

"Objection!" John yelled again.

\*\*\*

"Dad, Dad!"

John O'Malley sat up in the church pew, dazed at first, and then realized he had fallen asleep. Beside him, his wife, Mary, shook her head. "You are so embarrassing," she whispered.

"Dad, you yelled, 'Objection.' Everyone's looking," his son, Thomas, said with a giggle.

"Sorry, guys," John murmured.

He looked up at the pulpit. John mouthed "sorry" to the minister and folded his hands.

"There being no further objections," the minister said, and continued his sermon filled with familiar images—of shepherds and sheep, and a woman about to give birth who had ridden a donkey such a long way to a humble stable, and a husband who never left her side.

John knew the story well, but somehow it seemed new.

"That night, a star in the sky showed what was most important. It reminds us that the road to heaven is paved with good deeds," the minister concluded. "Have a blessed Christmas, everyone."

The choir sang the final hymn as the minister proceeded down the aisle greeting the congregation. Still seated in his pew, John O'Malley pondered his dream and realized that sometimes a good deed can serve some while denying others, despite intentions.

The minister paused at their pew, "How's our county prosecutor, Mr. O'Malley? Objecting to my sermon like that. Was it something I said?" A smile played on the clergyman's lips.

"My apologies, Pastor," O'Malley said. "By the way, I hear you'll be needing a soccer coach this spring?"

The minister clapped him on the shoulder. "That's good, John." He pointed to the window, turning the attention of the entire O'Malley family to the window. "Imagine that—snow."

# THE MANATEE

*He* sat quietly on a beach chair just five yards up from the surf, with an empty chair beside him. The sea was calm, trade winds light, with no other soul in sight. A beach towel stretched out on the sand next to him held snorkel gear and a full nylon sack. High-rise condominiums towered behind him, and the Boca Raton Inlet was just to his left, its jetty stretching far out into the Atlantic. The boulders made good platforms for fishermen, while only seagulls and a few pelicans perused it for the sunrise. The tropics had been his home for many years, and despite the perils of hurricanes, sharks, fire ants, and fire coral, it was his version of Martha's Vineyard.

The man stood up and grunted as he bent over the beach towel, picked up the mask, and placed it over his head. Then he picked up the nylon sack, full but light like a pillow, and tied it around his waist. He walked into the surf, slid his fins on, and dove forward while keeping his arms back. As he paddled along the outer side of the jetty, the warm water felt good, and lack of gravity eased his arthritic joints. This was his morning jog but with a far better view.

As he looked down toward the bottom, first to ten feet, then to twenty, he passed a batch of coral where schools of clown fish and angelfish loitered as a sea turtle passed by. Tropic waters had far more perils than Martha's Vineyard's, but he knew the terrain. Reef sharks would be feeding at the mouth of the inlet but, like alligators, they normally had no interest in humans—just the ones who got in their way.

As he rounded the end of the jetty, a school of mullet flashed by while pursued by a tarpon, and a reef shark passed in the distance with no interest. He wished he had brought his camera as he had on prior occasions, but his hands were full this time with the contents of the nylon sack.

He cleared the jetty and turned into the inlet, grateful to have caught the slack tide and not have to struggle his way in or out. He felt the water grow cooler and heavy, a testament to the lower salinity of the Intracoastal.

Finally, he reached the Intracoastal and lifted his head above the surface to spot the first boat dock where his friend spent most mornings. He waded toward it until he saw her shadow just beneath the surface, then lowered his head back into the water. There she was, a manatee massive in size and at least a thousand pounds, with a nursing calf beneath her fin.

At first she hung still before slowly approaching him, and as they drifted toward each other face-to-face, he smiled. He could see recognition in her calm, dark eyes. They drifted up to the surface together until her whiskered walrus-like head broke the surface with his. The man reached down into his nylon sack and pulled out the first of several heads of romaine lettuce for the manatee to chomp down. He gave her another as a pleasure boat idled by with a little girl looking on in fascination. They waved to each other, and he was sure the girl wished she could join them.

As the manatee chomped down the final head of lettuce, the man gently petted the side of her head while looking into her calm, dark eyes for a final time. Slowly, he turned away and paddled back toward the inlet.

After he rounded the end of the jetty and turned back toward the beach, a curious reef shark got a little too close for comfort and then moved on. A school of barracuda swam by as if on a mission, always grinning with those sharp teeth. The small-fry clowns and angels over the coral patch marked his path halfway in, and a sea turtle seemed to join him and then turn away.

When close to shore, he stood in the water to remove his fins while looking at the towel and two beach chairs in the sand. The second was for the one he had spent a lifetime with. When he viewed them as empty, he felt sad. But when he saw them as a pair, side by side, the sadness left.

Gravity set in as he stepped out of the surf onto the hot sand, relieved that his arthritis felt better. Now he was tired and hungry—the good kind of hungry, for bacon, ham, and eggs.

He folded the beach chairs, gathered his snorkel gear into the nylon sack, and started back to his car, but while walking along the edge of the shoreline, he stepped on something painful. It was sharp, like a wasp's sting. He stumbled to the ground and turned his foot upward to see that a piece of fire coral had punctured through his sole that had turned scarlet red.

"Dammit!" he hissed with the first spoken word of the morning.

"Oh, poor baby," a voice said softly.

He looked up with recognition into calm, dark eyes and raised his hand as if against her cheek. She was still with him, and no footprints in the sand were needed.

"Damned fire coral got me," he said. "Sharks and barracuda out there with no problems, and I have to step on fire coral."

She nodded and smiled. "Poor baby. Let's get some breakfast. It's good for the soul, you know."

# FRED'S SHORTCOMINGS

*Whoosh* . . . whoosh, the aluminum pole flexes from my hands to the rake head on the bay's bottom. Its steel teeth pluck clams into the basket a dozen feet below the surface. The pole is an extension of my arms for farming the bay's bottom. Oyster shells and quarterdecks pile on deck, still needing to be culled, and while the wind is due north over open waters, waves are small and the boat rocks gently. It's a good day for jerk raking.

My flat-bottom skiff has a fifty-horsepower outboard with a small cabin mounted by the stern. The insides are battleship gray, the outer hull navy blue, and the bottom is covered with "red lead," copper paint to repel barnacles and seagrass. She's built for jerk raking, small and quick enough to return upwind for yet another pass over a bed in the middle grounds.

This catch comes in shades of blueish gray, while yesterday's was chalky white, coming from the sandy flats off Fire Island. Clams are spectators. They don't say much, but their shells speak volumes about their origins. The chalky-white ones come from sandbars, the blueish-gray ones from a blend called sugar bottom, and the dark-ash ones are plucked from the mud. Working mud is a messy business I like to stay away from. Cleanup's a bitch, and the clams seem depressed as if they always knew they were trapped in a dreary place.

"Sit Down, You're Rockin' the Boat" plays over and over in my head as I jerk the rake. I don't have much else to think about but a tune. I wonder, where's Fred?

Something falls from the sky and hits the deck with a sharp crack. I drop my rake handle and jump to the side. A seagull swoops down and picks up his shattered clam and jumps to the bow.

"Good morning, Fred," I say.

He ignores me as he pokes his beak through the broken shells like a surgeon and then gulps down the meat.

"I said, good morning, Fred, and I wish you wouldn't do that."

He's so rude, perched quietly on the bow like that without remorse. Seagulls are inconsiderate creatures. It's their nature.

I don't like to be ignored, so I turn my back and return to raking.

"Feed me," he says.

I ignore him, tit for tat.

"Feed me, Seymore...please!" he squawks.

And there we go. My name's not Seymore, but he said please. I pick a chowder from the pile on deck, break it against a cleat and toss it his way. He stomps it with his webbed foot, gulps it down, and then . . . "Feed me!"

"Dang it, Fred!"

I hoist the rake, dump my catch on deck, and send a few more chowders his way. I needed the break anyway. Finally, he ruffles his feathers, splashes some white poop on my bow, and turns his back on me—so rude.

"One of these days, Fred"—I go back to raking—"pow, right to the moon!"

"It's not as it appears, you know . . . that moon," he says.

Now he's talking—to argue, I'm sure. He only sees what's wrong and seems to find pleasure in this.

"People write songs about the moon," he says, "but it has no light of its own. It simply reflects the sun's light. Without the sun, no one would know it was there. That's not very romantic when you think about it."

Seagulls are both gregarious and antisocial. They flock together but bicker over everything—not just food and shelter but mundane minutia, like who perches where on an open dock. But I am not a seagull and prefer to use what I call "reverse seagull psychology." It works.

"You're right when I look at it that way, Fred."

He hops along the side of the boat and stands beside me, his head perched back as if surprised. He's never come this close.

"You agree?" he says. "Yes, moonlight is really sunlight. You see it too?"

"Yes, the fools!"

"He's wrong, you know."

This voice was not Fred's. It had a higher pitch and came from below.

I look down at the pile of shells. An oyster shell flips

over, and a blue crab peeks out just enough to expose his face and a claw.

"I'm nocturnal, and the bird is wrong. I prefer to feed and mate under the moonlight, and that's romantic."

Fred freezes and cocks his head toward the pile like an Irish setter pointing at game.

"I see you!" Fred says.

"The bird will eat me!"

I scoff at Fred, "And you would, wouldn't you?"

Seagulls are diurnal and always hungry. So I pick up my bailer, the top half of a plastic Clorox bottle I made to scoop bilge water. Then I gently scoop up the crab and return him to the bay, where he darts down out of sight.

"You eat them too!" Fred says in disgust. Seagulls have such angry eyes.

He flies to the bow and turns his back on me, silent once again. So I go back to raking.

There's something about Fred. He's abrasive and rude. He wants shellfish, and I know that's the only reason he's been squatting on my boat. He's not very interesting and has no imagination. Who cares if moonlight is the reflection of sunlight? He just wants to argue, and that's his nature. But he's company and I like that part. He takes my mind off me, giving a break from this solitude. And with a little imagination and seagull psychology, I can make the situation tolerable.

"You eat them too!" he squawks again.

"You're right, Fred. I'm sorry. I hadn't thought of it that way."

*Joe Roubicek*

## About The Author

After a childhood on Long Island and forty years in Florida, Joe Roubicek has "gone country"and enjoys his family in Nashville, Tennessee.

He was first published in the Long Island Fisherman at fourteen. A story about fishing in the middle of a blue-fish-frenzy off Long Island's north shore, and it was written during after school detention. He has been writing ever since.

He dabbles in both memoir, and fiction, and is currently working on a novel.

# Acknowledgements

My appreciation for publishing goes to the following literary journals:

Tricia at the literary journal FAITH, HOPE & FICTION for:
THE HIDDEN in 2023.
THE FIGHT CLUB (Incorporated into SWAN RIVER.) IN 2023.
THE GOOD PROSECUTOR in 2023.
THE HOUSE in 2025.

And the SPOTLONG REVIEW for
FRED'S SHORTCOMINGS in 2024.

A special thank you goes to my friends at the Walton Writers for their inspiration and friendship.